Daniel Staniforth

SKYLIGHT
PRESS

First published in Great Britain in 2011 by Skylight Press,
210 Brooklyn Road, Cheltenham, Glos GL51 8EA

Cover painting by Mikki Nylund: "Folk Dance in Brooklyn", Mixed
Media on Canvas, 2011.
www.mikkinylund.com

Designed and typeset by Rebsie Fairholm

Printed and bound in Great Britain by Lightning Source, Milton
Keynes

www.skylightpress.co.uk

ISBN 978-1-908011-18-3

For all the displaced, dislocated, dislodged, and diasporic that dwell among us…

HEY

I't's a long way from Hull and East Yorkshire, both in terms of time and space, and Yally often felt the pangs of separation. Those plain, colourless years living astride the Humber estuary, years he had sought to shed in questing the Atlantic, had a way of clinging to his memory, although perforated now by the remove that he had long sought and longer regretted. He couldn't say why; the time had been reasonable, and the situation faintly rewarding. It was just a soft commotion in the blood that bubbled every now and again, causing that backward glance that all pioneers are ashamed to reveal.

"Waste of time."

That would be Hugh in angry remonstrance, shrink wrapped in his tattered red Che Guevara shirt so that the imprint resembled Charlie Chaplin more than the stolid revolutionary.

"Too far gone – done for – the country will never freakin' change that way."

It was always said in a sort of guttural taunt – and not always intended in the direction it was hurled. The younger son, Hugh Yallum, was one of those convenience disciples who got more out of the tone of delivery than the actual portent of the words. Anarchy was the vehicle and revolution the ignition by which to fire it up. There were no real convictions: he was fourteen.

Helping empower youth, that's what it was all about for the immigrant that continually failed to quite acculturate to a new country. Henry was the consummate widower, revelling in the role, perpetuating the stereotype, each day a continuance of the sad pantomime. But it wasn't so much his deceased wife, Hilda, that he mourned but more so the loss of youth, the self-banishment from Kingston.

"November's coming up fast, son."

Late October always excited him as there was always one somewhere, usually in the local district, even at the library on the corner.

"*Uh is the sound that the mother makes when the baby breaks.*"[1]

Hal wasn't listening, being tethered as usual to a grey, second generation iPod. Where Hugh was the brawling postulator on the eternal ring of anger, Hal was the neat anchorite that loved his dingy cloister webbed with dusty electronics. Hugh let out steam where Hal sucked it in.

"Bloody hell lad, can't you give me a minute?"

Henry edgily yanked at the white cord and the earbud flew across the table.

"What now Dad?" Hugh countered testily.

"If you come in about ten, I can show you how the booth works."

"I got it Dad," he said, jamming the felted disk back into his ear in annoyance.

"You're both deluded," came a sharp speared voice from the other room.

"You stay out of it. You might feel different when you're eighteen. Bleedin' knowitall!"

And so it went on, this time-honoured exchange, except this time a little heightened by a deepening entrenchment that each of them burrowed into. Heighth and depth – Jung's archetypes and all that. Hal's stony indifference infuriated Henry, but not quite as much as Hugh's indignation. Of course, the two brothers were at inexorable odds at all times, complete opposites in all things, except perhaps the love of one or two bands, albeit at different times. But high election yield was the utter conviction of Henry Edgar Yallum and he was bound and determined to hold to such, and by some scramble of exertion pass it on to his boys.

He'd done a few over the years: officer, attendant, counter, ratifier, recounter, and exit poller. The State Board of Election commissioners knew him well enough that he never had to produce any certification upon reporting; he was just the fussy, slightly eccentric, and funny speaking man from down the road that always volunteered. Of course, there were others that always volunteered too, like old Mrs. Young with the brutish looking overbite that sent voters scurrying into the polling tents. He'd had a run in with her that first year.

"What do you mean you are praying?" he'd barked at her. "This is an election not a revival meeting. You're not praying while I'm here!"

The cheek of it! Such a thing would never have happened in the Humberside constituency, well at least when it was a constituency. That was done away with in sixty two, thank God.

"Church and state," he'd hurled at her just once and glared.

I've followed the bloody puritans here, he'd thought to himself while staring up at old Mrs. Young's scowling but slowly yielding defiance. But Henry was quite simply a man of rules, a meticulous set of regulations well formed over the years that could not be prevailed against. He knew that technically the law stood with him despite all the inroads taken at the behest of religion, their legions of infiltrators with fists full of holy voting guides.

"That's why we should tax the church." Hugh had barked this statement when hearing of the account. He was only eight at the time but was fast growing into his anti-authoritarian jackboots.

Home-schooling suited Hal, not least because it allowed him to liaise with the shadows of his quiet existence, untouched and untrammelled by the outside world, a world that always felt claustrophobic whenever he was caught out in it. He abided his father's rigid system of governance – and even the countless and oft-repeated stories of the old country. He quite liked the sound of the place and bristled when Hugh thundered through with his brusque and epigrammatic denunciations. Through the stuttering tales of the Humber-embattled "Yally," he had come to feel a soft admiration for the man his father once was, even if it was at odds with the obsessive curmudgeon he was fast becoming. He had agreed to vote on his eighteenth birthday, only because he knew that it was the best form of appeasement he could offer in order to stay in good graces and retain his preferred way of living. He wanted to keep the distant mutterings of college at bay and retain his ghostly existence in the quiet room at the back of the house.

"Sod that," his brother had intoned predictably at that moment.

If there was one thing he found useful about his father's cultural heritage, among all the castle prancing and court mincing, it was his vast array of delightfully sharp sounding swear words. Of course, Hugh was bitter about mornings in the makeshift prison of the schoolroom, while the other boys in the neighbourhood made for the public school bus. He had even torn up his dad's *Home Educators* and *Youth* magazines in proud training for the anarchist that he would later become. He was the first to utter those barb-tipped words.

"But why do you care Dad? You can't even vote."

In most immigrant families, such a statement would be met with sighs, temporary resignation, and that psychological shaking off that the disenfranchised do so well. But for some reason, a would-be revolutionary had managed to strike a blow in his first bumbling act of defiance.

"Will there be a curtain?" Hal ventured upon the awkward moment.

It seemed to be the most important detail for the virginal voter on the morning of his first thrusting act of civic duty.

"Yes but... what about the issues? Do you know who you are gonna vote for? Have you even looked into it?"

Such pointed questions always led to silence. Henry wasn't a man that hammered his point home, or followed it up with varying levels of insistency; the original utterance was always shaped to do its job. He was a deft guilt honer. A few moments of silence were only interrupted by the deftly timed nudging of a leaflet towards Hal's breakfast bowl.

"Get it down you lad."

"Not that one – my dad will be working there." Something that sounded suspiciously like a command was met with creased brows and pursed lips, especially as it came from the geeky home-school kid that they'd begrudgingly given membership to. Nevertheless, theirs was a covert mission so it wouldn't do to drag a parent in and make things awkward, even though such missions were rarely seen through to their planned goal. Youth for the Eviction of History was an odd mishmash group comprising long-haired skateboarding Che worshippers, half-hearted punk-rockers, suburban white gangstas, and one self-styled "Vato" from Peru. Hugh had worked long and hard, suffering all manner of taunts and abuse to get into the club, including the smearing of dog shit on the mayor's front door with his bare hands. He had lobbied to use a plastic bag but the initiation rite had been uncompromisingly insistent upon hand-to-shit contact, resulting in smeary swastika. Once again the new mission involved faeces, as the aggrandized plan of the young anarchists was to break into the polling station and leave their own unique ballots to be counted by the morning officiators. Imagine that Young upper lip at seven in the morning after the offerings had all night to percolate! Hugh felt a twinge of disappointment that his carefully sculpted profile was being subjected to so base an enterprise, almost to the point of embarrassment. The rendezvous was nigh and he even had a brand new set of cammies to break in for the occasion, but he hesitated in the shadows deeply irritated by his inertia. In the back of his mind he could hear his dad droning through one of his pet stories about how he was born down the road from the great William Wilberforce.

They had met at Great Yarmouth, and Hilda never imagined that it could be so bad 'just up the coast,' but rather went along with it – like the North Sea. The 'healthy early years' as he liked to call them didn't tug on her memory with anything like the sort of affability that he sanctioned them with. The second childbirth had been problematic and the hysterectomy that followed was botched by an inept National Health butcher who had evidently cut away far more than the fallopian rigging.

"We're getting nowhere here," she would whisper quietly to herself while staring out onto the Humber estuary yard works, feeling like her soul was being sucked into the indiscriminate silt marshes beyond.

"Nonsense, this is Larkin country this," he would say, or something alluding to some bygone sage that may have momentarily unhorsed there. "Besides, what would I do in America?"

But she knew it was just another tidal barrier to overcome, the boys had already cast their votes along with her, although the younger one admittedly in just a sharp affirmative grunt. The marriage was as ashen as the lurching sky and his regulatory demeanour somehow failed to note the slowing chimes of her mortality.

The familiar obstacles to venturing outside were all there as Hal lurched through the screen door only to close it gingerly and not very emphatically. It was not that he was a complete agoraphobe; he had learned to operate somewhat in the outside world but only in terms of occasional leisure; nothing with such a sense of purpose. Even though the walk was a matter of steps, there was the small possibility of encountering other late morning walkers along the sidewalk, which often precipitated the need for uncomfortable eye contact and the slight demarcation of acknowledgment. His father, of course, had made the same journey, albeit more positively, three hours earlier that morning – and it appeared that the scant voting population of the town had already made the trek, for the street was soothingly empty. As usual, Hal cocooned himself in his iPodular casing in order to anaesthetize any sense of awkwardness in the outside world.

"Come along and show me something that I never knew in your eyes. Take away the tourniquet..." [2]

His steps began to synthesize to the rhythm by the time he reached a small dithering line outside the polling station. He had half expected his father to be standing sentry at the doors, on the lookout for a wayward son that needed a stiff initiation in the arts of societal responsibility. But old Yally was nowhere to be seen. He took his place in line behind one of the shifty eyed librarians, who immediately turned around and coated him with a veneer of suspicion. He positioned his body so as not to share space and retreated into something more interior.

"You used to be so warm and affectionate. All the little things I used to hear my fairy say." [3]

He was transfixed to such an extent that he did not notice the small line being sucked through the station doors, making a mockery of his avoidance. When he did walk through the cold brass-railed doors, he was surprised to be confronted with a rather smug Mrs. Young, bottom lip subsuming the rest of her face in an absurd half-smile.

"Where's Mr. Yallum?" he asked unsurely.

"Been dismissed," came back a lispy but triumphant reply.

"What… why?" he stammered.

"Can't say why. There's a booth open on the right."

The moment splintered and broke down as he stared at her for a few seconds before vacantly shuffling toward the open curtain to his right, a cavernous space that should have pleased him but for which he wasn't prepared. He felt lost, discombobulated, inadequate, as if he were embarking upon something subversive and ethically challengeable. A polling station without his father was unthinkable; his first vote without the shadow of rectitude and correction hanging over him, implausible. The small booth felt restrictive, a retainer for the sick and the damned. He felt sown up inside a body bag with the last stitch coming for his nose. He began to panic.

"Calm down," he told himself. "Where's the ballot?"

The sight of the sheet on the high rise desk steadied him somewhat until he began to examine the contents. He was unsure of the names, the check-box alignments, the order of particulars, and each time he went to make his mark he withdrew his hand sharply, wincing and second-guessing each impulse. It was important that he reflected his father's political views, that he gave a political voice to the man that had served the process on both sides of the Atlantic, but he just couldn't be sure which was the right option, if there was a right option even. He hadn't studied the issues; the propositions made no sense, had no particular truck with his paltry existence. He had half a mind to guess, to go random, and to mark in reckless hope, in order to leave some trace, some semblance of affectation, some final gasp of citizenry.

"Damn, where is Dad?" he hissed before pushing the ballot book violently against the booth wall and leaving it in complete naked abstention. He exited the station in the fastest manner possible without drawing attention, pushed through the doors, and made for the first narrow alley adjoining the main street.

Although relieved to find the house empty, Hugh still slithered in as noiselessly as possible. He knew his chance had gone begging and that he was out of the clan no questions asked. No one had called; no one had inquired as to where he was, or as to why the would-be El Che was a no-show for his big guerilla debut. He knew no one would inquire either; he was a nonentity, an immediate fader, a mouthpiece with no substance, a shirt-filler, just another pasty poser choking on some cultivated anonymous anger. Come to think of it, he didn't even know why he opposed elections, or government, or kings, or traffic wardens. Oh he knew the standard reactions that his role demanded, or those that drew chortles and sniggers from the class. He loved the wide-eyed looks of disbelief that his one-liners caused, the open-mouthed look of wonder from Yvonne Hillman that gave off just a hint of affection when exposed to his antics.

"Anyone home?"

Hal had slunk through the open door, catching Hugh slightly unaware, but the usual desultory comment didn't come.

"What's wrong with you?" he quizzed.

"Nothing," retorted Hal, pivoting uncharacteristically away. "Where's Dad? He wasn't at the polls."

Hugh looked down quickly, immediately suspecting that his father's non-appearance had something to do with the YEH mission, that his former comrades had somehow gone against the original agreement and moved the prank back to the intended target.

"This is so unlike him," said Hal with an odd quiver in his voice.

"We should go look for him."

But where to start? Where would you look for a man normally besotted with routine and regulation? The brothers were suddenly united in indecision, frozen in a suspended moment when nothing made sense any longer. It was an odd but strangely binding sensation, eye to eye in the oncoming twilight, hostile energies yielding.

The stones faced east in haphazard fashion, no governing principle as to which were nineteenth century plots and which were twentieth. The older ones were ringed with algae along the dewy grass lines, taking on the hue of a mottled brown paper bag. But it was on one of the newer ones that they found him, one still neatly mounded with riblets of new shoots poking through mud. The air was as grey as the day, pungent with unspent drizzle, and low dull clouds clotting above the inscriptions. His forehead was creased by the outer angle of the headstone bout and his three longest fingers lay neatly in each of the letters that marked H.E.Y.

On Hal's iPod:
1 *Hey* by The Pixies
2 & 3 *Hey* by The Red Hot Chilli Peppers

Diddle Diddle

He couldn't believe it: he had pole position; it was perfectly placed, in the bag. He had the numbers, the media grazing at will on his repackaged and neatly presented version of 'family values,' the coy abstinence-only pin-up smile. He'd shifted the centre to the right, mollified the left-leaners with good old country charm, and pirouetted nimbly through the electorate minefield without a stray trip-wire in sight. Then suddenly – she.

"You can't run on a name like that," his best friend, Priestly, had told him. "It's political suicide – it smells like bad history, treason, and secular humanism – it will undo all your precarious Ivy League jockeying."

"What's wrong with Dudeldopp? This is a nation of immigrants you know," he had countered.

"Immigrants you run against. Immigrants you're trying to wall out with your social programme closures and your small government elitism. Why do you think you've failed in three races? Your name contains the antithesis to all your ideas!"

His father hadn't been that keen either. At first, he was an oiled spigot, pumping in cash from stocks, t-bills, corporate ventures, co-sponsors, prestige societies, and other sundry conglomerates in the murky backwaters of his fiefdom. But the drainage only extended so far, could only come from self-perpetuating sources, sort of like a seasoned gambler that will only play with last night's winnings. For young Dudeldopp this was always a source of mild chafery. He wanted the floodgates open, the house willingly waged, and more importantly the inheritance pre-appropriated in the spirit of family trust. He couldn't understand why the absolute demise of his father was necessary to preclude the precession of fiscal power, why one had to wither for the other to ripen. It was a constant source of irritation between Maude and himself, a thorniness that prickled at the edges of their marriage, never quite letting them get close.

"Why can't the old crust cut you in now? It's not like you're ever going to need it more is it? Here you are on the verge of greatness, a far grander greatness than he's ever been able to muster in all his dealings – and he's holding out."

And so the comments often ran, hissed from the twisted right corner of her mouth. He could see them forming in her feigned public smiles at white-glove events. He could feel them piling in the ever-growing gulf in the middle of their king-size bed. With her, it wasn't 'in sickness and in health' – it was 'in trickiness and in wealth.'

"It's some stipulation in his will. I suppose running for congress on all his values and winning doesn't make the grade does it? You know how he is with secrets."

Connie had come out of nowhere – literally nowhere – just appeared. He had been very meticulous about all his appointments, from campaign manager to ad designer to intern, all were subjected to ruthless criteria before being selected. He had been a stickler about getting married people in – well married people with a civic profile or at least no divorcees or remarried types. It was important that the posse around him reflected his values, old fashioned, battle-tested values that had served as cornerstones for the Republic. These had to be people of certain faith, of local colour, of proud heritage, of spotless character, standing against the invasions, the infusions, the intrusions coming from the other side.

"Why are you settling for less?" she had simply and quietly asked when first catching his attention. He had stared at her for a longer moment than deemed appropriate in meeting a woman twenty years his junior. He had been caught between pure physical captivation and the distant need to place her genus, occupation and origin.

"Erm … less?"

What followed was a blur now because somehow she had neatly sidestepped his cautiousness and need for control, blithely wriggled into the first semblance of his confidence as if casually trying on an evening gown. He could not say at what moment, or by what means she had done this, only that she had done so emphatically. Connie Mann was some mystical amalgam, part statistician, part planner, part marketing whiz, part social networking expert, but mostly a sinewy enchantress that embalmed him with her liquid touch. With subtle craft and artifice, she quietly eclipsed his coterie of stepford wife administrators, his toadying male shoulder-warmers, and his value-clad lobbyists. She'd convinced him that he had overlooked a whole demographic with his ill-advised campaign tactics, and that the very people that could deliver him the staunch anti-immigrant vote were why, the immigrants themselves. This meant that he had to expand the canvassing, enlarge the buttressing, re-vamp the blustering in what amounted to a grander vision. Priestly had been against it immediately and saw it as an advance upon his chief-advising position.

"I don't understand the need to change trains now. We're winning. We've got this thing sown up," he had insisted, arrowing his gaze sharply on the unruffled Ms. Mann. Maude had been more ambivalent on the surface.

"Well perhaps it's a way to get the old sot to loosen the purse strings, although I don't see why you have to blow it all on trying to win by a bigger margin."

Old man Dudeldopp, of course, had found the whole thing preposterous.

"Winning is only meaningful if you win by inches," he had grunted. "I thought I had taught you to calculate the exact amount you need to seal the deal, not pour money in to just pad the victory."

At first he had begrudgingly consented to widening the expenditure, kicking off with exemplary pledges in order to ensure bigger matches. But as the campaign had worn on, he had grown tired of seeing his added investiture not being met with electoral gains. If anything, the race was tightening, the polls showed a slight, but worrying all the same, turn. Then something snapped, a retainer wasn't paid, a state dinner was cancelled as the distinguished guests were assembling, and the first whisperings of rumours quietly snuffed out the candles on a once robust campaign.

Despite all the trappings of the shadowy affair, Dudeldopp somehow sensed that he was also part of some well preserved and choreographed tradition. He couldn't say that he was completely caught out, that the trap was well hidden and the motions furtive, neither could he say that he wasn't aware of the usual destiny of such participation. When the flirting became overt, when the first delicate touches came, when the shadowy corners were sought for a potentially lusty rendezvous, he knew the endgame. As the numbers dropped, the righteous rhetoric sharpened, and the bodies slumped beneath the plumbline of family values, the outcome could never be questioned. The precedents all looked on like anxious ghosts do on a man that won't succumb to their haunting.

Who's to say when the first card fell, what moment began the precipitation to collapse? All he knew is that Maude's twisted smile began to more resemble a snarl. Priestly's jockeying suddenly became less jocund. The old man's credit became less creditable. But worst of all, Connie sidled out of the invisible side-door from whence she had come. Then there were the whispers, the return of the old ghosts, the campaigner's curse – to be met with that special stare reserved for all public hypocrites. There was the falling away of staff, corporate financiers, entrepreneurs, partisans, moralists, co-religionists, precipitating the wholesale peeling away of the electorate. The news stories ran, hands were rubbed, lips were lipped; there's nothing quite like a widescreen wake for the fallen. But as the last card teetered, the clause was invoked, that grand spindle propping up a lifetime of secrets had shattered under the paper weight.

How was he to know? She – his own half-sister? The victim was now paraded in front of a row of sympathetic TV cameras, pregnant, publicly pondering abortion or adoption. He had willingly gambled prosperity, the life to be gained – but now had he lost the life he had earned. She had diddled him twice.

"You can't run on a name like that," he whispered, disinherited and alone.

The Cat And

"What time did she say she'd be here?"
"Round about midnight."
"Seriously TC."
"Seriously, after our first set, or thereabouts."

The Cat's Meow was starting to thicken with chatter, fill in with the usual neighbourhood miscreants, give or take a few new faces. And always loved that pre-gig feeling, that last warm whisky while staring at the instruments on stage, those moments of anticipation before the night's tone was truly struck. A couple of his 'ladies' were sauntering off to the side, women on the cusp of middle age, past child-rearing and flirtatious games, the 'in and out' set. The Hepcats appealed to the worn and the downtrodden, reviving the analogue sounds of bygone days, hazier days when the Cat's Meow was thick with smoke and a white boy's jive was still fresh on the tongue. Miles and Diz were still alive then, and zoot suited swingsters were making a short-lived comeback. The Hepcats played through the revivals, through the neo-fad and old-hope couplings, outliving them all in their willing pastiche.

"Ready to go And?"
"It's TC in here. We're in game-mode."

Top Cat, as he insisted on being called, tossed back his last preparatory shooter and slid off the barstool.

25

The gigs were more or less the same revolving affair; the odd change in solo perhaps, an extra coda even, but the songs played themselves – strung along by habit and history. The repetition was fine as long as one found "the zone" – that self-inflicted purgatorious space that cared neither for elation nor damnation. It was the automated dance, the pre-ordained music of knowing fingers and lips, subservience to the canon that is Jazz. They had seen off the Stray Cats, the Pole Cats, the Rat Catchers, the Purr Snatchers, and all manner of feline musical appendages. The audience shared the same sense of fixity, bopping through the changeups and solos, finding their own erogenous zones in the listening act. It was the music of the guttural and instantaneous, worn down like the grainless oak floors, yielding up the ghosts of passive sound travel. Every great once in a while he would feel the lilting gait of a Mazurka or Polonaise subsumed under the rhythm, like an eclipsed moon biding time under a chosen void.

He hoped she would come in during "Turn Me On" – or at least "Run Away with Me" but the well lit doorway yielded up no late shadows. How many times had he psychologically prepared to sing a song to the tardys and the no-shows? His was an act mirror-perfected, artfully crafted with all the hallmarks of the great crooners – and yet so many performances in the vacuum. He'd first noticed her during "In a Sentimental Mood" – alas one of his zoneless renditions that he worked hard to salvage when she slinked in with her large eyes swimming the room. He knew right away that this wasn't one of the usuals, the "last call" regulars that would try and entice

26

him and his earnings to some poorly furnished loft. This was one of the new hipster brood with a purposeful arrival and some honest inquisivity for his craft. He had made his initial approach casually.

"Who's the new sinner lady?" He had asked somewhat pompously.

"Too bad you ain't no black saint," came the blanchless reply.

She knew her Mingus then, probably her 'Trane and Monk too.

"I'm Top Cat," he tried more conventionally.

"Are you really ... top?" came the flirtatious response. Truth be told, he was relieved when they didn't buckle early, the tension sharpened his wit, shaped his performance. He was able to get into the 'zone' when the changes were challenging, tricky, demanding. He loved the call and response, the pure contrapuntal nature of the initial stand-off, even the fear of being outplayed. They had jostled all night, rubbing and chafing, hinting and purring, circling and flexing. Yes they had warmed, touched even, but sexless, like the reedsman fingering a mute scale well before the solo. There was something dark and shifty, weightless perhaps, in the way she augured around him, in a manner that would not betray any intention. It was the slow Chodzony dance from ancient world, one that lurked beneath new syncopations. She would be here tonight and her round promising eyes at the moment of declaration had haloed his presence ever since.

As the last half-wrought encore withered into tired silence he surveyed the room. No sign of Mia. The

Hepcats collectively slumped into that nightly funereal rite of winding cords and packing up instruments when the doorman came in with a shiny red package.

"Left at the door for you TC."

He knew from whence it had come the moment he touched it, still warm from her hands, or at least he wanted to think. He took it to a far table, turned his back and slid his finger between the seams. Soft, velvety, an apologetic token perhaps. He pulled out what looked to be pyjamas, dark blue with different silhouetted cat poses throughout. A blank envelope wafted to the floor and he quickly retrieved it. Perfumed? He couldn't tell in the slush of nocturnal barroom aroma but he wanted to think it was.

Dear Topmost. I wanted to keep our engagement but last time I had this strange reaction to you. Could it be that I'm allergic? Please accept this clumsy gift I made for you. Just one of those things. M.

All the experiential slinking in the world couldn't quite prepare one for this and he just sat there staring at the dark shapes.

"Coming And? We're going for a nightcap at the usual."

"I'll be along boys."

The Hepcats played on as always, through the blues-sharpened disappointments and abandonments, that was the point wasn't it? Topcat crooned on, always inventorying the strewn tables in hope, always averting his gaze when it was met with bland acceptance. He

wore the pyjama top as a shirt under his lounge jacket –
he had tried to find her at other clubs, music mags, local
colleges, instrument shops, and even the hair salons. She
had dropped him off with a mere song reference and no
amount of certainty in his soul beforehand had done
him any good. Allergic? The crassness stung him as he
cut away his goatee, the dark spirals of dander floating to
the floor.

The Fiddle

He wasn't sure where they were all coming from, the seekers, but they continued to crop up like beetles out of some porous brick. He'd already surpassed the old opportunity schemes by some distance, and surprisingly so, as it seemed such a far-fetched idea with no attached clues as to supply and demand.

"Yes, they are imported."

Which was somewhat true, although he left out the bit about the Chinese origins in order to sustain the supposition that they were legitimately from Norway.

"How do you play all these strings?" was a question that always seemed to come from the uninitiated. Those in the know knew that only four strings were playable, the rest being resonantly sympathetic – as was Sander to the uninitiated. He preferred the culturally curious, or the inquisitively ancestral customers, as they tended to take things on face value and not ask delving questions. They weren't true Hardangers, or Hardingfeles as he painfully learned to call them in a confrontation with a real Norwegian. But it's not as if they were cracker boxes either. It took some considerable skill – and he had to rely on his six month apprenticeship as a cabinet maker back in the days of honest youth. The scrolls weren't right for one thing; far too stubby and made for the conventional four strings of the classical violin. He got them 'in the white' as they say, naked, unvarnished and undrilled. Bored smaller holes, and filled them with soprano uke pegs, pipa pegs, dowel rods, anything. Then there were the graduations. A traditional violin is a real piece of lumber, much too solid to get that whispery Norse echo. It took a fair bit of scraping with a spoon gouge, then a block sander, whipping through millimetres towards some half-baked notion of authenticity. He modified old warped viola bridges to accommodate the extra strings, sometimes doubling, tripling, according to the gradations of customer ignorance. Then there was his favourite bit, the customized ornate purfling with spirals and arrows, some inner tribal begging for classification beneath the varnish.

Then the Harding-fellow came back, asked testing questions about the placement of the understrings, or the legitimacy of the paper Hardanger Fjord label, says he's a member of the HFAA and knows a lot of people from the old country.

"Kvint, kvart, ters, bass…"

A knowing head bob came with his every plucking of the string. Sander, of course, knew how to play the unperturbed, the quiet expert that wisely forebears some fuss around his creation; the omniscient allowance. He knew how to stay in the game even when caught unaware, how to spin nonsense into plausible authority. He had spent time and cunning on his forged Norge and wasn't about to let the first blasts of real Norsk unravel him. The trick was to keep the statesman's repose while plucking the goods from one's adversary, make the man answer his own questions then give the quiz. He'd milked more than a few pyramid schemes this way, stayed at the table long past the first raw deal.

"The spacing is off, should be point five at the bridge."

"Yes, it was made originally for a small woman's fingers."

"But this is wider than point five."

"Well she had a touch of dropsy and the shakes."

"This is no good for gammaldansmusikk."

"Her name was Gunnhild Marit."

"That's a type of Norwegian music."

"Yes, she played the Inlander variety."

"Perhaps a slattar," he said striking the strings with his hand.

"Yeah she was a bit."

And so the conversations ran, which at least kept him from working in the presence of this inquisitor. Always probing with giant pauses between their statements, one trying to catch the other out, the other trying to out the one catch. Soon it became an afternoon game, always the same hands, the object to flush out the bluff or bluff the flush. Sometimes this gambler's jostle would play out in front of a third party, almost always one of the uninitiated.

"I'm one sixteenth Norwegian on my mother's side and I would like to connect with my heritage through music."

Such would be the table for the gambler's cards, laid one by one in alternating synchronicity. Sander would start simple and whittle away at his opponent's greater knowledge, but always finding a knot to expound on, a seam to fill. He had an artful way of working Edvard Grieg in, then it was free range from the Vikings to Sigurdsson to the Kalmar Union.

"Which instrument would you recommend for me?" would be followed by a duopoly of sizings, stylings, and intonings – one counteracting the other as the Hardangers piled up on the show-counter like the snaking Great Wall. That's not to say that it was all at odds, there was some give and take, some sham concessions and the occasional verbal backslap. It was the orthodox against the heresiarchan, the original competing with its simulacra, conceding inches to gain millimetres, a really fine show. Whether the fiddle was sold or not was neither here nor there, the creeping discourse was the thing.

Of course, it helped Sander immensely that there was no single authoritative tuning for the instrument, so when Harding showed off with his 'Troll tuning from the Valdres,' he could easily counter with his own 'Pixie pipe tuning from the Gyntlands.' The trick was to sound authentic, speak declaratively and insist on equal verisimilitude. Yes, he could have consulted his book on ethnic instruments, origins of the violin, Googled to his heart's content but that would have been cheating.

The Cow Jumped

It seems to be a rite of passage that at some point in anyone's youth, one will have to endure a sordid interim in the fast-food industry. Flipping burgers, slinging patties, chucking chuck, whatever you want to call it, was something most spotty teenagers were subjected to in preparation for something grander and more meaningful in life. The joint on North Vache Street was no exception, with its transient and oft-changing collection of Christians, perverts, pushers, filchers, straight-edge, gangstas, nerds, and immigrants. Jersey had worked there the longest of them all, outlasting the usual stay of pre-college service or any notion of upward mobility. The simple fact was that he had no ambition, drive, or verve anywhere about him, and the minimum wage pay packet fed his feverish video game habit.

The rookies worked the fryers, dropping reconstructed potato wedges and crumb-welded chicken strips into boiling vats of oil all day, commanded by a variety of beeps and buzzers. The normal sojourn at the fry station was about four weeks, give or take a few days for prolonged ineptitude or burns. There was also the weeding out factor, for many couldn't or wouldn't complete this obligatory initiation before storming out or plotting some grand exit to a construction job or office temp position. Jersey saw many come and go, and more zoom past him on the path to bun filling graduation. In his princely slackerdom, he thought he'd seen off the lowest competitors in the underbelly of burgerland, fought off any invasive claims to his prized position of supreme wastrel. That was until Dem came.

At first it seemed like Demissie would blow by Jersey and his perpetual fry status quicker than any other, being a generally bright young boy from Ethiopia with impeccable English and good manners. But the fact was that he was prone to long dark periods of the most morose kind, as if something truly haunting would creep up on him from very far away. These lapses in spirit would cause synchronous blips in performance, which led to many mishaps in front of the customer gaze. In periods where he was seemingly flying through the day, the clouds would gather and Dem would burn successive batches, dump a hot grease basket on the floor and splatter the backs of the legs of the register servers. He would slice a finger opening a frozen fry bag, blood sizzling effervescently in the hot oil. Or he would clatter into an assembler carrying a stocking tray of sandwich fillings. At first Jersey thought he was simply bipolar but that seemed to be too much of an American disease for his sharp fry-partner. No, it was something psychological and deeply rooted, something from the North African plains that had followed him here.

"Get that for me Dem."

"My name is Demissie."

Unlike other immigrants, who were all too happy to convert to a more American sounding name, or at least abbreviate their nominal utterance so that it suited the limited Anglo tongue, Demissie clung to his rather fiercely. Calling him Missie, or otherwise feminising his name, didn't have the desired juvenile effect, for it didn't faze him in the slightest. There had been Koreans named Bill, Ukrainians called Bob, even other African brothers that settled for Jim or Kim – but Demissie would not shed the one thing that made him instantly peculiar or other. Unlike the other employees who had cast him off as a slightly likeable but now vexing foreigner, Jersey decided to take a personal interest, as if it were one of his simulated role-playing games that kept him up until all hours. At first, there were no returns to his probing but their having a unique camaraderie in failure began to pay dividends in the currency of friendship. The trick was to maximize the light periods, gain as much ground as possible before the black and foul moods set in. This wasn't simply a case of working around chronic depression, this was a haunted maze, a labyrinth of demons to be circumvented.

He learned that Dem was from the Omo valley of southwestern Ethiopia, from a proud tribe known as the Hamer. Dem would talk with large glowing eyes about the river people and their fierce rivalries, the tribal games amongst the livestock, and their constant battles against the seasonal floods. The story would always advance joyfully with its teller demonstrating marvellous dexterity and timing with the wire baskets, only to run up against the shore of some internal dark ocean, which was inevitably proceeded by performance collapse, calamity, the topsy-turvy nature of which being the only thing that kept the poor boy in a job, in that his shift managers were highly and continually confused. Jersey tried to cultivate an after hours companionship, thinking that a change in venue, away from the frozen sizzles and burger flips, might unlock the next layer of the sanctum. Video games didn't work, held no charms, and thus were reluctantly abandoned for more stealthful pursuits. This involved the braving of new worlds such as libraries, street markets he never knew existed, strange games with stones, and a trail of secondary and tertiary relatives with similar names.

They were well past the normative fryer advancement time and Jersey had not made any real inroads as to his friend's dark visitations. It's hard to say at what point the moment of truth precipitation came, but one night when they were at a diner Dem went into a sort of a trance. At first it seemed that he'd been captivated by a sleek Hispanic girl three tables along, cheekbones catching the half light in animated conversation. Without diverting his gaze or even so much as a blink, he started in on an eerie mantra.

"The cow jumped over me. The cow jumped over me. I'm a failure. Failure."

Jersey tried to retrieve the situation through distraction, obfuscation, and eventually a sharp under the table kick, but the trail of strange words continued through a soft moan, almost like a novice at a didgeridoo. At first, Jersey wondered if this particular girl, seemingly unperturbed in a world far away, had any bearing on the situation, a past lover perhaps, an awkward rendezvous. But it soon became apparent that he was looking through her, that she was just a conduit to something repressed at a much deeper level.

The low moan suddenly stopped and Jersey felt his companion's bright marble eyes swivel back to the present.

"She remind me of my sister just before they dipped her hair in red clay, ochre, and butter. She look at me and say, Demissie – you become a man." Jersey began to shift at what he supposed might be coming, a grizzly death, or worse – a tribal rape. He began to wonder why he had got mixed up in dark things that could not be assimilated into his culture, his slacker ethos, his preordained gaming comfort where the levels were always projected in experiential layers. He wasn't ready for this thing out of left field or some shadowy Ethiopian river bank among emaciated bullocks. Stop the game, he thought, eject the disk and move on to something more familiar.

"She is sexy," he said vacantly.

"Who, my sister?" Dem rounded loudly.

"No, her." He motioned beyond.

Dem shook his head and then sat quietly for a while, seemingly in mid-decision over what he might say next. Jersey silently hoped that they would leave it on the periphery level, just checking a girl out, what boys are supposed to do.

"I am cursed," Dem said rather suddenly. "You stay with me, you be cursed too."

There was a long silence, distant chinking of plates.

"My own ceremony to be a man and I fail. All I need to do is run across the backs of the cow three times but I fall. I fall and the cow jump over me."

As Jersey tried to piece together the admissions, Dem rose to his feet quickly, looked over at the talking girl for a scant moment, then turned and walked out. Jersey knew he would by frying solo on the morrow.

Over the Moon

he little inner balcony at Malloy's pub was the usual place to pontificate about tactical nous, refereeing bias, and individual performance.

"Your number seven had a good game."

"Yeah – the lad is getting the hang of it. Coming out of his shell a bit too."

"Has he grown since the last game?"

"Shot up a bit yes. You know how they are at this age – one minute small, snotty, and squeaky – the next, towering and basso."

"Hope he stays with soccer."

"Football!"

"This is America!"

"This is football. We invented it!"

Pat Moon was the consummate British ex-pat; had a source for sausage rolls and lemon tarts, watched footy on satellite, and refused to drink Budweiser or any equivalent 'chemical bilge.' He quite enjoyed coaching the local 12-year-old boys, schooling them in the ancient and specifically 'global' wiles of the round ball, all the while chipping away at their well ingrained allegiances to American sports. It chafed him that his sport was seen as a recess sport, eclipsed by more manly games on diamonds and grids, and so often dismissed with a xenophobic wave of the hand. It all the more annoyed him then that his direct contemporary on the other side of the field usually consisted of some squat Neanderthal with no knowledge of the 'beautiful game', bellowing their ignorance across the field and smearing all and sundry with it. Bill was a specimen, all brawn and no brains, shoe-horning all sports into the same shallow ethos.

"Your number two is never a striker Bill. Try him at centre half."

"Well we creamed you so he must be doing something right."

"Well that's only because my regular keeper didn't show up and the back-up likes to pick daisies."

"Well, my non-forward managed to score a goal that no goalie would stop."

"It was a penalty Bill, you're supposed to score those."

"Yeah but it was a fierce PK all the same."

"It went in off the goalie's face and the post. He toe-bunged it right at him."

"It was a good punt, admit it."

Pat hated losing to such lack of artistry, to stumbling ignorance on the back of shameless luck. He hated it more so now for the traditional coaches' get together at the Balcony, where the gloating was going to be incessant. Gibbs slunk up to the table with his usual perverted smile.

"Oh yeah boys. Another shellacking. Four nothing and top of the table. How did you get on?"

"Three one."

"What, to the limey?"

"No, to the US."

And so the humiliation continued and Pat had to quaff it along with his bitter ale. Bill and Gibbs were all about the scoreboard and in support of whatever Machiavellianism principles needed to win, the hell with skill, training, and embetterment. They didn't even know the proper position names. I mean, what the hell is a half-back? And what decade were they in with their mandatory sweeper for every game? But worse by far was the incessant whooping from the sidelines, bludgeoning the poor kids for ninety minutes with all manner of invectives spewing from popping neck veins.

"Oh by the way, Carter is outside. He wants to see you."

It was odd for the league administrator to be around Malloy's. Pat wasn't even sure if they knew about the after game ritual, much less where the best pseudo-British pub was. He had a swallow left in his ale. It would be a welcome reprieve from boasting cretins posing as football coaches.

"See you in a bit then lads."

Carter was another ape of a man, made to look even more ridiculous in that striped monstrosity that passes for an official's uniform in this country. He hadn't had many dealings with him and it was odd to be approaching him in a half deserted parking lot on a late Saturday afternoon.

"Sorry to chase you down Pat."

"No prob. Anything wrong?"

"Well... er... this is not easy for me. I'm afraid I'm going to have to ask you to leave the team."

"What, just because we lost to that jammy lot?"

"Not exactly, I think it… I think it may be a lifestyle thing."

"What the blazes do you mean Carter? I'm the best you've got."

"Well, it's just a bit strange. All the other coaches are dads too, so they have an ulterior motive for what they do."

"I thought you said that wasn't a problem. I just love the game. I love to coach."

Carter shifted uneasily on the tarmac, obviously trying to twist the conversation around to something more specific, all the while hoping that Pat would accept his marching orders before he had to get to the heart of the matter.

"Pat… how do I put this. I think you may be of the wrong persuasion."

"What, being English? Voting Social Democrat? Liking astrology? What the fuck are you on about?"

"It's just that your ulterior motive for being here might be at odds with our mission, or with the comfort of the parents."

"No parents have complained, not to me at least. Why just last week one wrote me a nice thank you letter for the Aston Villa scarf I brought back from my last trip home."

"Er… I know… and a few have said positive things… but there have been suggestions…"

"Look Carter, I don't know what you are mincing on about so just come out with it. What's been said?"

"OK then. It's just come to my attention that your

particular lifestyle choice might not be suitable for coaching young boys."

"Are you saying I'm gay?"

"You're not?"

"Course not. And what if I was? Whose been saying this stuff?"

"It's not important who, and we've promised confidentiality. It's just that certain people feel that there has been some inappropriate touching."

"Touching? What? Who? This is outrageous Carter. Did those idiot coaches put you up to this?"

"I'm sorry Pat. I have already contacted the parents and told them that I will take over the team until another suitable coach can be found."

"Suitable coach? You'll ruin the team. You haven't got a clue. You're as gay as I am!"

"Sorry Pat. If you come around the fields I will have to file for a restraining order."

"But this is preposterous. You're sending me off because you THINK I'm some child molester? And I thought your penalty decision couldn't be topped!"

Carter swivelled oddly, walked towards the pub and up the stairs. Pat stood there staring after him, shaking his head disbelievingly.

In the fields beyond, the familiar clash of young legs, boys like bees around a hive.

The Little Dog

All weddings suffer from moments of panic but not the sort produced at this particular wedding. It was the moment for the ring, the moment where the mistake generally happens if it is going to happen, and of course it did. Jorge and Rosie were on the sharp end of the promise waiting for the time old symbol to be produced, to seal the deal so to speak. In ancient times, a circular instrument was placed through the noses of hogs and women to subjugate them. In this more modern case, it was a dog, or what was believed to be a dog, that held up the union.

"It's gone. He's gone. *Se ha ido,*" came the cry from the best man, which prompted 30 suit-clad men to drop to their knees and search for a matchbox.

At first, Carlos was horrified as the entrusted bearer but as he began to swish around the Astroturf style church carpet, he began to harbour secret feelings that the sacrifice might be worth it; that the loss of the beast might be worth the temporary embarrassment of the not-quite-weds, even as a painful stain on their memory. It was one thing to own a temperamental hairless Chihuahua, it was quite another when that 'dog' was a baby rodent sized runt that had to be ferried around in a box or on a small cushion for fear of it being squashed underfoot or prey to a slightly bigger animal.

For a fast acculturating Mexican family, Poco had been an immediate delight despite his awkward dwarfened state. Already full grown and neurotic, the little Chihuahueño had appeared to howls of pity and slight feelings of nostalgia, the breed being named after the state of their ancestors. Both Jorge and Carlos had taken to it right away, including the strange novelty that it was a dog that couldn't be walked, wrestled, or plied with sticks and bones. There was something infinitely precious about it regardless of its ugly, diminutive, and slightly deformed appearance, something more ancient than the Azteca. They took turns in carrying it around, impressing girls of different ages, including the highly affable Rosie who once lodged it pathetically in her cleavage. They began to wear shirts with top pockets, create small elastic leashes so it would spring back like a yo-yo upon escape. They each paid it a lot of attention, fighting over it, handling it, and building elaborate obstacle courses for it out of the smaller children's toys. But as with all boys and their toys, they soon tired of it and began to seek less tethering pursuits.

It was soon after, under Rosie's adoptive care, that Poco had his first seizure.

"*Oh, Dios mio.* What is it doing? Is it dying?"

The entire family rushed over to witness the bizarre scene of a hairless miniature dog writhing on its back like some upturned beetle, snarling and groaning as it tried to furrow into a cushion. Carlos brought over a small meaty kibble to see if that would appease it, and

Conchita tried to put its favourite tin marble between its paws. But it wasn't until Rosie softly ran a finger along its spasmic body that it slowed to a luxuriating stretch and let out a long eerie moan. There was something about the dilating black eyes and the semi-erotic purr that made each of the family members wince and look up at each other.

This strange epileptic episode was followed by others, all coming with slightly different symptoms and affectations. There was the incessant growling that only could be stopped by instant coddling, then the destructive scratching that demanded a finger behind the elephantine ears. Such outbursts began to test the familial fortitude and tetchy arguments would often follow after Poco had achieved his desired ends. Rosie, who more and more got stuck with the task of mollification, became increasingly spooked at how the little beast would bear its dishevelled teeth, accompanied by a low drone growl and quivering lips, until she would be forced to stroke its smooth skin. She began to see it as less of an animal and more like an unwanted appendage, some growth or tumour that had grafted itself upon the family she was planning to marry into.

"*Usted está mal*" she would whisper to its relaxing snarl. "Little devil. *Pequeño Diablo.*"

The moan would start like a soft siren in the middle of the night, crescendoing until someone got up and took Poco to their pillow. Of course, this caused resentment as turns were missed, shifts were avoided, and the fetid, stale smell of the tiny beast caused bad dreams. Eventually, Jorge convinced Rosie to keep it at her house, as she was the one that Poco seemed to respond to the most, seemed to need the most. At first, this caused a small resentment and opened a tiny pore of doubt upon their hopes for a happy marriage, one that slowly enlargened and grew rancid. By now Rosie had to endure the snorting lump a few inches from her face every night or the bone-jarring whine would start and she would have to touch it again. Such nights began to breathe a certain foulness upon her waking demeanour, the size of which could surely not come from this pulsating scrotum-like animal on her pillow.

"Can we give it away? Get rid of it? *Por favor?*" she cried at her wit's end one day. "I can't take it any more."

Nevertheless, she struggled on, doggedly going through with the marriage plans despite the canine interruptions. In the days leading up to the wedding she appeared almost stoic, the tension easing, as she administered to Poco's needs with a growing automated manner. The feast was prepared, the mariachis booked, the décor perfected as the guests began to pour into the Church of the Immaculate Conception.

The ceremony was eerily uninterrupted, strangely pleasant, when the moment called for the ring. Carlos had played with it the night before.

"It's like a finger collar, or noose," he had thought.

"It's gone. He's gone. *Se ha ido.*"

The male guests began their crouched scramble, sifting across the floor like crabs in search of a little box. They listened for the famous drone, that ancient wail that had made their hair stand on end.

"*No hay problema!*" cried Rosie. "We have a back-up."

The men, including Jorge, scrambled to their feet as Rosie produced a plain white gold band that caught the afternoon sun. The Padre thought he recognised the peculiar look in Rosie's eyes and married on.

Laughed to See

It was on a night like this that Irene loved living by the ocean, a lucid night that held the weight of ions bursting upon the million shingles. There was something about lying in the bed with the pearlescent moon peeping through the chink in the curtains, all the while orchestrating the roar of the incoming tide. It was a singular happiness lying there next to her dead bulk of a husband, riding the nocturnal crash and drag of the sea. Tides of memory slung up against present; Aquaduct beach staring out to Ceasarea as her childhood retracted. She let out a soft chuckle, stifled it, and turned on to her side to welcome oblivion.

The Tates normally ate a simple breakfast, nothing too fancy but ritualistic just the same, and allowing for them to take in more mental sustenance, her at the laptop and him at the morning paper. It wasn't unusual for Nick to be tickled by something in his morning news digest and he chortled just the same this morning, except that something seemed to catch in his throat and it turned into a violent cough. Irene, although concerned, as one would be, found herself smiling just the same.

"Got something down the wrong hole then?"

"Something about this obituary struck me as particularly funny; an old fisherman survived by his wife, Shelly Steele."

"Oh that is rather Ironic."

As was customary, Nick tottered off to the car and mentally prepared himself for another trying work day, fully detesting his job, only to double back rather boisterously.

"I forgot my keys... ha ha ha!"

He certainly was in a good mood this morning, she thought. Unusual for a Tuesday, the likes of which were usually laden with heavy plodding and sighing.

"I wonder what's got into him," she thought, suddenly imagining all sorts of scenarios; affairs, a drinking problem, early onset senility perhaps.

Irene went about her normal Tuesday ritual, as her schedule was carefully compartmentalized by time and the strict adjudication of tasks, from which she rarely wavered unless beset by depression or guilt. The hanging calendar bore its dutiful portents as she surveyed it over coffee. Yes, it was time for changing bed sheets and paying the mid-monthly bills, including the phone, Amex card, and the first payment on the deductable for the Optometrist. Although one might think her obsessive and irrepressibly organized, Irene wasn't a complete workaday, just preferring to get her work out of the way early so that she could relax to some afternoon television, chat sites, or walk along the promenade. The latter was at the vigorous urging of her therapist who believed that her chances of a complete recovery were vastly improved with daily brisk walks and good sea air.

It was odd for Nick to call mid-morning as he was a known despiser of all things relating to phones, and even stranger considering his demeanour. When she picked up the phone he was laughing but he suddenly cut it off to speak in a quite serious tone.

"I left my lunch on the counter."

"Are you alright dear?"

"Yeah, rough day. Boss is riding me hard."

"You'll have to get something at the corner deli but go easy, I just paid the bill."

"Is it Kosher?"

"As far as I remember."

There was a longish silence, punctuated by a rustling and what sounded like a stifled moan.

"Are you at work?"

"Yeah... sorry, just had to sneeze."

"Perhaps you're coming down with something."

"Perhaps. See you in a...."

The phone cut off abruptly and now she was heavily suspicious. That did not sound like a work phone call, as rare as they were – and there was something dishonest about his voice. Where could he be? And if not at work, where? And why would he call?

The phone rang again.

"Nick... Oh."

There was a woman on the other line with one of those starchy professional voices, the kind you hear on political survey calls or from collection agencies, polite but faintly cutting. This must be her, Irene thought, she's calling for him.

"This is Hilary from Dr. Rolle's office, calling to check up on Mr. Tate."

"Oh... this is his wife, Irene."

"How's he doing, any complications after the procedure?"

"No, he seems happy with the contacts. He's even reading again."

"Anything else?"

Irene was caught slightly off guard as the question seemed to point to something beyond the bounds of the phone call. Was this really a doctor's assistant?

"Er… no. He was saying just yesterday that he was thrilled to have his eyesight back."

"Very good. Well, do call if anything comes up. This is a new stem cell culturation procedure, so we're trying to follow up any new data."

As she lowered the phone, she tried to imagine putting on such a phone call but the stem cell bit sounded legitimate, especially now that she remembered him mentioning something about the procedure. His eyes had been bad since birth and she'd become used to his thick lensed glasses and the way he peered over them at his newspaper. Come to think about it, something about his mild clumsiness and slow focusing stare had attracted her to him, as if he was always distracted by her, always striving to hold her in his attention. She remembered the agonizing period after his laser surgery, the bitter disappointment that his corneas could not be corrected by this expensive breakthrough lasic procedure. Months of depression had followed, framed by stacks of unread newspapers in the garage, when suddenly he stumbled on yet another hopeful procedure. At first he had been reticent, as had she. Yet another medical vacuum to suck away at their lower middle class income.

She was startled when he came home early that afternoon, something that he never did unless there was some earth-shattering reason. As much as he despised his job, his work day was as regimental as her chore-bound mornings. Perhaps he hadn't gone to work at all. There was that phone call, his strange behaviour, something was amiss.

"You're home early."

He paused at the doorway, uncertain of whether to come in.

"I got suspended."

"What? Suspended? How can... what for?"

"Inappropriate behaviour."

His head dropped with the last syllable and she thought better than to press immediately, giving him time to compose himself. Besides, she was in slight shock too. Whatever had happened was obviously serious enough to break him up and she'd rather let it bubble up to the surface naturally than apply unnecessary pressure. Such was their marriage. Suddenly, Nick looked straight at her and let out a violent full-bellied laugh but definitely not the sort that followed humour. His eyes were sharp and lucid and the bellow blasted through the house, breaking off as bruisingly as it had started.

"Nick, you're scaring me!"

Again, his eyes sank and he began to shake, obviously in the grip of something spasmodic and uncontrollable. At first she thought he was going into a seizure but he managed to right himself, albeit still shakily, and make his way to the loveseat.

"Something's not right."

His voice complied with his statement, for it sounded hollow and yet constricted, nothing like the voice she had lived with for seventeen years. Irene slowly gained control of her own entrammelled spirit and went to comfort her husband. She ran her fingers through his short sandy hair, which seemed to calm him and steady his breathing.

"What is it?"

"Dunno."

She made him herbal tea and managed to get him to eat against his will before the second blast of involuntary laughter came, then the third. No matter how many times it happened, or how commonplace it became throughout the evening, there was no way to process it for either of them as they sat in the burst silence that followed. In the intervals they dared to talk, they considered emergency rooms, sleeping pills, brusque walks, internet searches but neither could actively escape the inertia that comes with shock and foreboding.

"It's something to do with my eyes."

"What? How?"

"Dunno, just is."

"Actually, they did call today… to ask how you were doing."

"Mwha hahahahaha!"

"Nick!"

"I'm scared too."

"I wonder if there is a way to reverse it."

"No reversal."

"What? How do you know?"

"No reversal, that's what he said."

As they sat there and stared at each other, he took in all her immaculate details as if for the first time. She was smooth, porcelain, kibbutzim glows with soft shadows in all the right places. The Doctor had told him that it would be shocking, this latent revelation of details up until now unseen with such clarity and precision. He remembered the odd remark as he had fitted him with the particularly filmy lenses.

"You might find you want it back."

"What back?"

"Your myopia," he said laughing.

Such Fun

It had gone on long enough, some thirteen years now. It was time to finish it, thought Solcher as he made his annual painful roll out of the crumpled hippodrome, over dewy bits of Knödel and cups half full of frozen Bock froth. It was time to move on, assimilate, shuffle off his German beer corpse coil and do something more meaningful with his remaining half-life. Of course, he'd said that last year, and the year before, in much the same way, while plucking the Oktoberfest flotsam out of his lederhosen and declaring "Well, at least we don't do the full sixteen days," then finding a fresh place to throw up. He'd almost gone through with it last year, almost fired himself the morning after, only to be talked around by the Chairman of the Parks and Recreation Events Committee.

"We don't have another authentic first generation Bavarian Solcher. And besides, your festivals are such fun. No one can put it together like you do."

He'd gone home with a mind to mull it over, assess the opposing forces that annually stirred within him, give it an honest perusal between moments of honest purging. There was always that state of uncertainty when the field was strewn with Brezn, vomit, and the odd flattened Tirolerhüte but then the Parks and Rec

61

cleanup crew would come in and make the place pristine again, thus renewing his dependency. Then there would be the growing glossalalia around his performance; "best yet," "Epic," "München would be proud," and so on, that would spur on a repeat performance. Of course, these loud blasts of praise would almost always be followed by soft whispers; "mad kraut," "Hofbräu-head," "betrunkener," which was slightly unnerving. He knew that within a few decibels he went from crown-prince Ludwig to clown-prince Spass but somehow the latter never quite completely detracted from the former.

One couldn't quite make a living from the measly stipend for one event so Solcher had to endure planning many lesser events throughout the year. He oversaw the Valentine picnic, the Easter egg hunt, the fourth of July mini-fireworks display, the Halloween ghost walk, the Thanksgiving turkey roast, and the Christmas light parade – with the usual smattering of weddings, bar mitzvahs, revival meetings, protests, park plays, and music nights in between – but there was no doubt in the town that Oktoberfest was the premier event that no one in a breathing state would miss. Quite simply, it was a feat of unparalleled planning that even the properly Germanic towns nearby couldn't begin to compete with, so they permanently folded their tents and came in bus-loads. From the histrionic gun salute at the first keg tapping, to the authentic array of food and ale, to the slowly crescendoing Schlager and the brightly costumed dancing, Solcher's historische wiesen was crafted to precision, a miracle of Teutonic timing and staging befitting of the Father-land. This is not to say that it was just the deft trick of yearly repetition. Solcher often tore up the script, redesigned the sets, and variated the festivities. One year, he worked in a troop of amazing dancing puppets that disappeared one by one to the 'umpah' of the music. Another year, he choreographed a bombastic scene from Wagner's Siegfried Idyll to fireworks. He'd even managed to recreate a Lugwigian horserace in the early years. Given, it was more of a donkey trot with hired midgets, but the costumes were fabulous and it got the Steins clanking to a steady rhythm. So there is no question as to the success of the festival, or to the dashing veracity of its planner. Even the debauch that Solcher would unerringly drive himself to each year had become part of the annual attraction, at least on the night. And yet the thought of another year drove him to despair.

Thus, the annual hangover came and despite the perfect trappings of his masterpiece, Solcher felt something slipping away. It wasn't the morning after titters that necessarily vexed him, or even the dishevelled state in which he had spent a rather public night. There was something troubling about having to simulate his own authenticity every year, as if the show were for him and him alone. In truth, it was the only remotely German thing he did any more as the language and the alpine memories withered within him. Can a perfect simulacrum be a substitute for the real? Did his progression from carefully monitoring the drinking to becoming a bona fide Bierleichen represent some form of dying? Did his cultural-missionary zeal truly mean anything to a five acre field of thrill-seeking Americans, hopping from one cultural holiday to the next? Last night had been especially bitter as the perfection had become rancid at an abnormally early stage of the evening. He was slurring before dusk and had his first stumble before the Kranzerl Polka, a dance for which he had always been lucid. Something irked him more than usual about the half-hearted exchanges of pidgin German, or the way people fed their Limburger cheese to their dogs when no one was looking. He felt a new disdain for such cultural reduction on a day he'd always intended as expansion.

"Mr. Shloss, I've decided to tender my resignation. I can't do it any more."

"Now look Solcher we do this every…"

"I know we do. But this time I'm deadly serious."

"You're just hung-over. Call me tomorrow."

"I'm afraid there will be no tomorrow this time, Mr. Shloss. I've…"

"Nonsense. You can't leave. We don't have another authentic first generation Bavarian Solcher. And besides, your festivals are such fun. No one can put it together like the great Solcher Spass, not even the Germans."

The next day, as always, Solcher sat around in his soiled tracht transfixed in a mixture of guilt and humility. It was a yearly ritual, this coming down, like the child-like sombreness the day after Christmas. It was a bit more pointed this year, or at least it seemed to be, thought Solcher.

"Not even the Germans," he said quietly to himself. "Not even the Germans."

And the Dish

The Digital Information Sky Highway van was always a gear too high even though it was an automatic transmission. Elena was used to the high grind and the displaced lurching that came with it, her body knowing how to brace and yield with balletic precision. Actually, it was the only true kinetic experience in her day, the rest of it going to a steady script with a fairly predictable dramatis personae. The drive, although physically imposing, gave her the opportunity to drift within the strange choreography, find alluring dream states that pulled from amalgamic phases both past and present. Today she thought of Kasos on the edge of the Eastern Aegeans, where she had often gazed through the perforated mist towards the dark rim of North Africa. She remembered the searching lips of a dark stranger at the Agios Georgios monastery, or at least revelled in the possibility. But alas, the Dodecanese reverie dissipated as she pulled into a well worn driveway shaped like a horse-shoe.

"Mr. Stumbel, it's gone out again?"

"Can't get hafe the chaynels."

His drawl was impenetrable but she was determined to draw out words and meanings, learn nuances, grasp the shapes and colours that surrounded American

English. In the early days she despaired at such visits to 'repeat customers,' was leery of their intentions, the machinations behind their readied smiles and beckoning gestures. She was aware that she was a rather attractive woman in a trade that was traditionally prescribed for men. The early days had brought depression and a lacerated sense of self-worth, which wore heavy on the manual living of a working class immigrant. She had sought to retreat into silence, to create a dark cavern of remove between her and her aspirants. But she found this to only catalyse their sordid sense of conquest, to stimulate the cheap-gotten wishes of the flesh. With her sorrel curls, Turkish hue, and sharp enamel eyes, all attempts at retreat were simply seen as erotic coyness, an invitation to the dark dance in the shadows. She couldn't play to the self-deluding orientalisms found in white male sophistry but she had found another tack.

"You need new dish Mr. Stumbel."

"Bob… call me Bob."

"Line of sight no good Mr. Stumbel, and these disecq switches need replacing. I tell you this last time."

"Well maybe ah wanted a secon' opinion."

"Same as first opinion. Same readings on LED meter."

Stumbel was anywhere between thirty and fifty five and in that particular state of mid-western disrepair. She had no idea what he did for a living, or did all day, and knew that he was well married despite his feeble attempts to obfuscate the signs. He liked to stand over her, working all the particular angles in which to appraise her womanhood. She knew it irked him that she wore the traditional overalls, just baggy enough to require his embattled imagination as to her approximate shaping.

"You really need to take care of wires. Too much crammed, then you will have fire Mr. Stumbel. Why you not take care of your things? This is expensive equipment, cost much to replace. Maple need trimming outside, cut off Eastern sky then you can't watch your games."

At first, her voice was pure sex; the rounded lilts and trailing off phonemes all through a perfumed breath from some exotic place. But she talked so god-damned much and always hinting at his failings, filling each musical sentence with subtle invectives about his performance, his virility, or lack thereof. But oh how he wanted her, doubled and tightened with desire at the mere hint of her, creased and crumpled within heretofore unknown regions of his craving.

"Local oscillator frequency too low. Digital package transmission no good Mr. Stumbel. It like a big block on your system, can't eat, can't shit, so you all full up! I keep tell you to upgrade system but you don't want to listen. You don't want buy new component – but cost you for me to come and tell you same thing every time. Viaka! I knew man like you when I work for Antenna GreekSat. He pay me to drive to Chalcis and tell him same thing. What your wife say? She like pay me to talk?"

The mere allusion to his well-hidden spouse had its desired affect, his calculating eyes diverted and he reduced himself to a more drawl-recessed mumble.

"Ain' merrid."

She estimated his wife to be roughly one and a half times her age, socially dishevelled, and gender-culturally subservient. She was probably loyal, principled, out working some demeaning job traditionally intended for sequestered mid-western women so that he could loaf at home. She noticed that he affected a limp at certain junctures of their typical conversation, but at other times pained to present himself as the picture of health.

"Can't you git the dern thing working?"

"I can bootstrap and you get half channels fuzzy. Then you pay me to come tell you same thing next month. Soon dispatcher say nothing we can do until you buy new component."

"How bout a drink, sugar?"

"I no drink sugar, no drink ferment sugar while I work. Beside, I have to go across town to see Mr. Malling."

"What that ol' goat want?"

"Same thing you. Pay me to talk, say same thing."

"Well he can wait awhile kennee?"

"Here's bill Mr. Stumbel. Have good day. Don't jam up CI slot this time."

As she lurched out of the horseshoe, she caught a glimpse of him sniffing the air where she had been, his finger propping open the curtains. She thought of Anieli, the way she had left him, pawing the air as she drove away to the airport. She felt the clefts beneath his collarbone, still imprinted from when he had last held her. Her shoulders now yielded to the shudders of the van, and to the tremors of her American dream.

Ran Away

It wasn't like BigTop to be gone this long. Sure, he'd often scarpered for hours at a time, and sometimes quite far afield, but never two days. Chase had also gone past the point of no return, at least some five, six miles from his house, and well into dusk. He'd beaten his previous exploit at any rate. He must have been seven or eight, planned his grand exit for at least two days, plotting and scheming, only to be gone twenty minutes or so before the cold January wind sliced through his resolve. He'd never quite worked out why he wanted to run away, or what the particular pressure was that lead to his meticulous packing of food and utensils before sneaking through the back gate. His home was normal enough, at least in some non-linear way provided a modicum of warmth and what passed for love between non-adepts.

"He's gone away to die. Had one like that at Muskee's, lifelong friend to all, only to slip away at the end. S'pose that's what we all do, slip away."

Mama rarely referred to her former life at that second rate circus, now that she had escaped from it all and settled down to some semblance of respectability, at least for a single parent. They didn't even have a decent elephant and the acrobats were always missing holds and catches from what he remembered. Every now and again the old life would resurface, when his Mama had too much Chianti and decided to walk on her hands, unbefitting of a paunchy Italian woman in her early fifties. Gravitational embarrassment to where even BigTop had hid his head.

"He's not going to die and I'm going after him."

"Capisco… only to the step-gate and be back by sundown."

He found himself taking the direction he'd taken all those years ago, head full of fierce independence and the verve of an escapist. He'd got to the field that time but then the shapeshifters came, the nocturnal choirs of misplaced marsh-ghosts wailing through the brush. The chill of the open space had surprised him, the grunts of unseen animals had unnerved him – and within seconds of foot-stomping assurance he had turned, walked, then ran back to the bungalow, through the maze of empty bottles, and into the bed of his unconscious mother. He was well past that now, past the field and its mixilating ethers, past the far copse and well into Smother's farmland.

"BigTop. Here Boy!"

He called, somewhat timidly but with a tone that he determined could be heard within a half mile. It was one of those pastel nights, where the moon was in a late wane, casting all with a strange iridescence, almost unworldly. He was thirteen, five years on from his previous excursion, well advanced in method and strength, almost full-grown he surmised. He thought of his dying pet, lying pathetically in some spiritual shadow, slowly breathing up the ghost, slowly releasing through pain and shudders. Why didn't animals die socially, surrounded by their likeness, cushioned in comfort and whispered encouragement? What if he was dead already? What if he was back there, already corpsified, part-corrupted in a dark mass, petrified in this unnerving moonlight? Should he go back? Should he retrace his steps to see if he'd walked past last the last gasps, the slow upward roll of eyes he had many times gazed in? But something led him on. Something cajoled him through the last boundaries of their daily walks to the unknown fields beyond. BigTop had provided the seam to slip through, the last hem before the nakedness of the future. He stopped calling.

Chase still faintly remembered his father, a silhouette that came and went at intervals, and a second-half act that never quite convinced the audience. He had been a clown, was still a clown for all he knew, still contriving to fall and injure himself for a few sterile laughs while the audience anticipated the high wire. He was the performer on the vision's periphery, the one you occasionally glanced at to see if there was any change to the state of mass pity, the one you grimaced through, willing the last joke. *"Cavaliere errante,"* Mama would call him. He couldn't remember him without the clown-nose, nor without the smear of hastily cleaned-up make-up. Indeed there was something smeary in the memory's residue. He only remembered two words being said, and those in a sort of tight alien voice.

"Ran Away."

And with that he stared into the middle distance,

everywhere and nowhere, with not a trace of searching recognition in his eyes. The few times he had come around since that had not been punctuated with words, only the scaling of walls and the slithering in and out of windows. He remembered the look of guilt in his Mama's eyes, the sort of look he imagined BigTop might have while pushing out his last exasp in the dark. "*I gran dolori sono muti*" whispered through the final sigh.

Chase came to a dark hedge-apple row, too thick to push through with neither end in sight. He walked along it looking for weaknesses, a place to find purchase either high or low, all the while hearing a dull roar beyond. He knew he'd reached the A27 interstate, which gushed even at pre-dawn hours. North would take him to the state line and the idea of changing states appealed to him. Does one change with the passing of boundaries? Is American Mom different from Italian Mama? He'd always been amazed by the amount of limberness she retained going from state to state, condition to condition. No matter her slight ballooning in girth, there was grace in her small movements, a bit of a pirouette swagger even in states of drunkenness. He had often caught men half her age transfixed by the fluidity of her subtle manoeuvring, agape at the roundness of her mechanics, the lines of supple grace about her gait. He wondered if he had inherited any of that, the movements that magnetise the gaze of the wilfully imprisoned beholder. Or was he the shifting torpor that was his father, the escapist who only attracted that momentary look that the least of nictations can distract?

BigTop had felt a strange presence within, a new passenger in his carriage that weighed him down in gallons. He loved his little family, coarse as they were, unshining as they were, but something in him told him that he had to leave. The dark presence was enlargening, taking over, and his act was done. He knew there was a way out, a loose pane in the old pine fence that he'd always known about. It hinged at a push and created an aperture as such that a determined dog could push through, a strange birthing that he had resisted up to this point. He knew that this was not normal for one of his kind, for most would have pushed through long ago. But he liked the company of the swerving lady that sometimes took to walking on her hands, or the brooding boy that had found a way to stare deep within his soul. For yes, he indeed had one, darkening though it was. And so one morning, with his newfound heaviness, he heaved his aching bulk against the weak spot and it yielded as he had always known it would. He followed the old route to the dark clump at the far end of the field and found a black hollow in an old ash. As he waited for the heaviness to subsume him, he heard his name in a shy but recognizable tone.

"BigTop. BigTop."

He felt a shadow come near, which took the coldness and the weight from him. As the silhouette moved on, he released his soul and shrank back into the hollows.

Chi be vive, ben muore.

With the Spoon

It was indeed a strange relationship. Just last week he could remember cradling her in his midsection, the small of her back slightly arching away from his navel, the points of her shoulder blades softly burrowing into his flesh around his nipples, as they watched the snow thicken on the larch. And now, the harsh angular intrusion of fresh anxieties, faintly threatened notions of restraining orders and midnight move-outs.

"I've told you a thousand times, don't use those. Those are 1890 expo edition silver, the real thing, not for you to bang around on like a moron!"

This had been the catalyst for the new spat, one of many that flared and rumbled on like one of those industrial trains with its endless line of lurching coal cars. This one seemed particularly elongated, with the steel on steel shrieks and grinds wearing away the parallel marital track.

Biff, or "Bones" as he preferred to be called, was one of those wiry, nerve-ransacked irritants that always had to be in motion, and always had be the producer of sound, as if his life depended on it. She would let him drive because his incessant drumming on the dashboard was slightly more animated than his thrumming on the steering wheel between turns. His was a percussive life and language of unending rattles, clanks, gongs, twangs, tonks, bumps, thuds, scrapes, where everything was a drum or a guiro, something to produce rhythm. At first she had found this charming, alluring, and oddly erotic, particularly as his metre and manner were natural to some metronomic core.

"I can prove to you that I'm a legitimate son of the Emerald Isle," he had said to her, then producing two bleached pairs of convex sheep bones, which he then held like ingrown claws between his fingers.

"This is where the spoons come from," he declared before producing a samba like rattle while gyrating his hips in tight little ellipses that drew her in. She then discovered that he had a fetishistic collection of spoon-like instruments, from moulded plastic to what he declared was iron age ore, to match her own. Hers was a positive monomania; souvenir spoons from every hamlet from Florida to Maine, New York to San Francisco, as well as a burgeoning assortment of international spoons. For most collectors, the craze had been popular in the post-war years, fizzling out when local smithing lost out to the cheap labour markets of Asian manufacturing. For them, buying a labelled collection from some disenchanted collector on Ebay didn't hold the same charm as trawling the length and breadth of the country and siphoning a cultural treasure – spoon by spoon. But Tina had no qualms with the more Machiavellian approaches to collecting, ruthlessly seizing charm spoons, photostone spoons, limited edition spoons, figurine spoons, Dutch porcelain spoons, royal silver spoons, location spoons, commemoration spoons, and on and on. She'd once flown to London just to get the jump on a dying man's collection of Paddington Bear spoons, elbowing through rows of undeserving relatives to get to them.

"Nothing but a poor man's castanets," he liked to tease, rattling away on a pair of cheap nickel plated Hiltons. She didn't mind his jibes at first, especially as he had a use for her poor auction buys and knock-off jobs. He was also fond of quoting a line from Eliot's Long Song of J. Alfred Prufrock.

"I have measured out my life with coffee spoons," would come rap-like to some clink-laden syncopation.

"Wouldn't that be tea spoons dear? You are making him Irish!"

"Nope. Coffee it was – and he was a Yank like yerself." *Clanger-clank-kerkling…*

It was these staccatoed correctives that began to wear away at some inner layer within her, like a spoon gouge whittling away wood. Something about the meticulous precision of his beats, how it worked in counterpoint with the surety of his emendations, it was percussive scraping on her fraying nerves. It was about the time that they went to visit the Claes Oldenburg sculpture in Minneapolis that her thoughts turned decidedly blacker. He was, of course, rattling through a precise redress of geometric curvature and proportion, pummelling away at her giant spoon moment, even adding a coda on the necessity of the suspended cherry. At that moment, she envisioned him crushed beneath the stainless steel spoon base, cherry-red blood staining the polyurethane enamel as she walked nonchalantly out of the sculpture garden. It was a turning point; something had stirred in her subconscious which now seethed like lava. When she read of the giant cooking spoon in Bavaria, she wondered if it could be wielded and how many strokes would complete the bludgeoning.

Although Biff conducted himself with a meticulous sense of self-certainty it could be said that he was starting to jounce on the inside, the outer vibrations eating back to some nerve-centred source. His rhythms began to speed up, not through an improving sense of technique or dexterity but because of some inner tightness that wound up his mechanism. At first, he too had been seduced by the fastidious order of things – and the no small painstaking passion around her well plotted agglomeration. He particularly loved how she held things, measuring weight and density against the bone. And the way she gently polished away the tarnishes, pursing and breathing against the silver with a low whistle. But as her collection grew, so did the annoyances and the chaferies that surrounded the accrual. The obsession slowly ate away at the savings, slowly eclipsed all the few other pleasurable nuances in their marriage. As sure as the display cases consumed the walls, her fixations on expansion swallowed her attention. He began to resent these non-practical pieces of dainty and decorative cutlery and schemed up new uses for them.

"When's enough gonna be enough?" he asked as she pushed a tray of ivory teaspoons up the wall.

"Egg spoons, demitasses, saucier ladles, soup spoons... bleedin' caviar bouillon dessert spoons...

horn spoons… runcible spoons… pickling spoons… rattail spoons up my arse… There's nowhere to sit any more!"

He did that thing with the bones of his thumbs while verbally rummaging through her collection that drove her mad. She wanted to shove a sporf through his eyeball and smash her Victorian slotted across his cheekbone. At the same time he wanted to dig into her cranial cap with that his old burnished absinthe spoon, and jab at her face with that gold mote spoon that hung by her chair. Thus they stared at each other for a long time, spoon feeding on small gestures of violence, he click-clacking forcefully, and she fingering the double bowl of the Welsh wooden spoon that had been his first gift of betrothal so long ago.